CAPTAIN FACT'S

HUMAN BODY ADVENTURE

BY KNIFE & PACKER

EGMONT

KNIFE & PACKER FACT!

ONE SUMMER HOLIDAY KNIFE AND
PACKER CAME DOWN WITH A MYSTERY
ILLNESS THAT COVERED THEM IN
SPOTS. THEIR DOCTOR TOLD THEM NOT
TO WORRY AS IT WASN'T CATCHING...
AS SOON AS THEY WERE BETTER KNIFE
AND PACKER GOT A NEW DOCTOR!

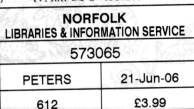
First published in Great Britain in 2005
by Egmont Books Limited, 239 Kensington High Street, London W8 6SA

Text and illustrations copyright © 2005 Knife and Packer
The moral rights of the authors have been asserted.

ISBN 1 4052 1769 3

3 5 7 9 10 8 6 4 2

A CIP catalogue record for this title is available
from the British Library

Printed and bound in Great Britain

CONTENTS

STAR

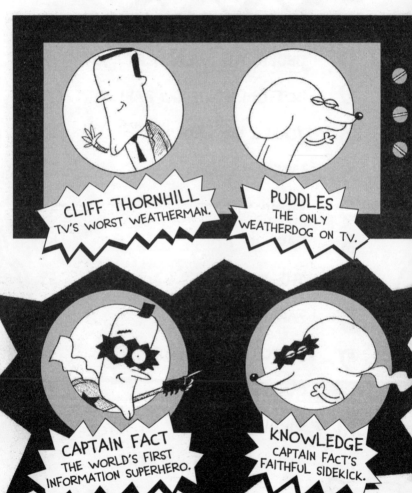

CLIFF THORNHILL
TV'S WORST WEATHERMAN.

PUDDLES
THE ONLY
WEATHERDOG ON TV.

CAPTAIN FACT
THE WORLD'S FIRST
INFORMATION SUPERHERO.

KNOWLEDGE
CAPTAIN FACT'S
FAITHFUL SIDEKICK.

RiNG...

LUCY
HEAD OF MAKE-UP AND CLIFF'S BEST FRIEND.

THE BOSS
HE'S SCARY!

PROFESSOR MINISCULE
HEAD OF THE FACT CAVE AND THE BRAINS BEHIND MISSIONS.

FACTORELLA
PROFESSOR MINISCULE'S DAUGHTER AND ALL-ROUND WHIZZ-KID.

CHAPTER 1
UNDER THE WEATHER

TV'S WORST WEATHERMAN, Cliff Thornhill, and his sidekick, Puddles the dog, were having a bad day. It was Cliff's annual medical check-up and Nurse Scalpel was in a foul mood.

As she pulled on some extra large and very squeaky surgical gloves, Cliff shuddered.

'It's days like this when I'm grateful to be a dog,' whispered Puddles, who had to keep his voice down in public.

'I've been prodded, pounded and pummelled – and that was just my tongue,' moaned Cliff.

As Nurse Scalpel swung round and loomed over Cliff, there was a knock at the door.

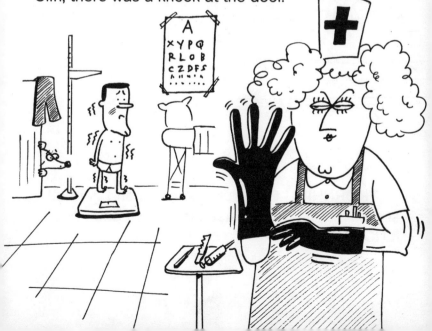

'Stay right where you are, Cliff!' barked Nurse Scalpel as she opened the door.

It was the Boss, and he was looking decidedly off-colour.

'THORNHILL! Get your clothes on and get out!' screeched the Boss. 'I need treatment and I need it NOW!

As Cliff thankfully left nurse Scalpel's first-aid room, he found most of the studio staff queuing for medical attention.

'I didn't know the whole studio was having a medical today,' said Cliff.

'We're not here for a medical,' said Errol the cameraman. 'We've all come down with boils . . . on the bottom!'

'On the *bottom*,' said Cliff. 'Now my medical doesn't seem so bad after all.'

As Cliff wove his way through the throng of sickly colleagues he felt a hand on his shoulder. It was Cliff's friend Lucy from the Make-up Department and she was out breath.

'Have you heard the news?' she gasped. 'There's a mystery virus on the loose – some sort of mutated superbug!'

'That explains the queue,' said Cliff. 'Is it affecting the whole city?'

'Worse than that – it's affecting the whole world! It's a global epidemic! From Anchorage to Australia, from Zurich to Zanzibar, people can't sit down. Doctors have never seen anything like it before and are powerless to help.'

'That sounds terrible,' muttered Cliff. 'But . . . er . . . we have to get the evening weather forecast knocked into shape.'

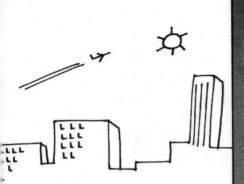

Cliff and Puddles dashed off to their office.

'What is it with Cliff?' thought Lucy. 'Half the office has been hit by a mystery virus, the world is in crisis and all Cliff can think about is cumulo nimbus and strato cumulus.'

But as Cliff shut the door to his office clouds were the last thing on his mind and Puddles knew exactly what was going to come next . . .

'This is a mission for Captain Fact!' Cliff declared, and with that Puddles pulled the lever to reveal the pole to the Fact Cave . . .

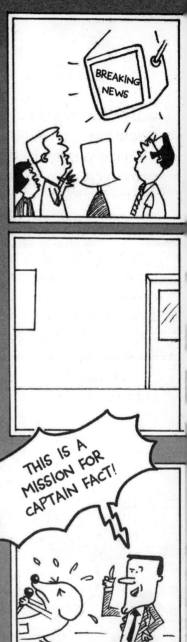

CAPTAIN FACT

KNOWLEDGE

13

'Keep up,
Knowledge,' said Captain
Fact as they hurtled down one of
the Fact Cave slides. 'This is going to push
us to the limit. We'll have to get up close and
extremely personal with this mystery virus if we're
going to save the world.'

'Can't they just zap it with a laser?' asked
Knowledge, who wasn't too keen on the idea of
meeting any sort of virus, let alone a mystery one.

'You don't just "zap" viruses,' said Captain Fact, 'let alone a superbug.'

'Well, won't they go away if you ask them nicely?' enquired Knowledge, hopefully.

'Listen, Knowledge, we're dealing with a mystery virus here, not unwanted house guests,' said an exasperated Captain Fact, as his shoulders began to shudder . . .

'How up close and personal are we going to have to get?' shuddered Knowledge.

'I did say extremely,' said Captain Fact as they landed at the door of the Nerve Centre.

CHAPTER 2
BOTTOM BOILS GO BALLISTIC!

'THERE YOU ARE!' said Professor Miniscule, the world's shortest genius. 'The mystery virus is getting out of control . . . so far people are only being affected in the backside department but if we don't do something about it soon the symptoms may become more serious.'

'You mean the virus could be . . . fatal?' asked Captain Fact nervously.

'We just can't take that chance,' said Professor Miniscule ominously. 'The medical profession has tried everything, but they can't work out whereabouts in the human body the virus has its HQ.'

'I think I know what this means,' gulped Knowledge.

'You superheroes are going to have to become micro-heroes,' said Professor Miniscule, as he brandished the world's most effective shrinking device, the Shrinkotron 2000. 'You're going to be injected into a human body to hunt down that superbug.

We need to know where they're hiding out and we need you to scan a live specimen. As soon as we have the information the doctors should be able to find a cure.'

'I'm not sure if I want to go into a human body,' said Knowledge nervously. 'It's going to be yucky in there. Mucus, snot, poo . . .'

'. . . Earwax, saliva, wee,' continued Captain Fact as he turned a shade of green. 'What could be more icky than that?'

But things were about to get a whole lot ickier, as Professor Miniscule pulled back the screens to reveal the body they were about to enter . . .

'THE BOSS!' exclaimed Captain Fact and Knowledge at the same time. 'GROSS-OUT!'

'Why him?' pleaded Captain Fact. 'We spend all day at the office trying to avoid him and now you want us to go *inside* him?'

'We needed a specimen suffering from the virus, and when Factorella and I went up the Fact Pole into your office he was the first person we came across.'

TA-DAA!

'He was so scared of Nurse Scalpel he'd run out of the first-aid room and then fainted outside your office,' said Factorella as she bounded in wearing a wetsuit. 'Dad and I had a job on our hands carrying him here. He definitely needs to cut back on the pizzas. So, when are we going in?'

'Factorella, I appreciated your help shifting the Boss,' said Professor Miniscule sternly, 'but you know fine well you're too young to go on missions.'

And with that he took aim with the Shrinkotron 2000. There was a bone-shuddering bang, a flash of blue light and before Captain Fact and Knowledge could say 'spleen' they had been shrunk.

Our two micro-heroes found themselves perched precariously on Professor Miniscule's fingertip.

'While I prepare these two for insertion, why don't you activate the Fact Cave supercomputer, Factotum, and show us what you've got on the human body,' suggested Professor Miniscule to Factorella as he set to work . . .

THE BODY IS MADE UP OF SYSTEMS.

THESE ARE PARTS OF THE BODY THAT WORK TOGETHER TO CARRY OUT VITAL TASKS. HERE ARE JUST SOME OF THE MOST IMPORTANT SYSTEMS:

DERMAL: SKIN IS THE OUTER LAYER OF OUR BODY THAT PROTECTS US AND HOLDS US TOGETHER!

SKELETAL: BONES PROVIDE THE STRUCTURE THAT THE WHOLE BODY IS BUILT ON.

DIGESTIVE: THIS SYSTEM TURNS FOOD INTO NUTRIENTS THAT KEEP OUR BODIES GOING.

URINARY: THE KIDNEYS ELIMINATE WASTE AND CLEAN OUR BLOOD. WHAT'S LEFT OVER LEAVES OUR BODY AS WEE.

RESPIRATORY: THIS SYSTEM NEVER RESTS BECAUSE WE NEED A CONSTANT SUPPLY OF OXYGEN TO STAY ALIVE.

MUSCULAR: MUSCLES ARE VITAL FOR ALL OUR EVERYDAY MOVEMENT AS WELL AS KEEPING US BREATHING AND DIGESTING.

25

Captain Fact and Knowledge were now in a gloopy liquid.

'These Multi-Purpose Oxygen Pills Professor Miniscule gave us are brilliant!' bubbled Knowledge. 'Apparently we'll be able to breathe in all kinds of fluids. But where are we?'

'We're in a hypodermic needle,' replied Captain Fact. 'Brace yourself, Knowledge, we're going iiiiiiiiiiiiiiiiiiiiiiiiiiiiiiiiin!!!'

CHAPTER 3
YOU'RE SO VEIN

CAPTAIN FACT AND Knowledge flew down the hypodermic needle and into the Boss.

They landed with a tremendous whooshing slurp. Everything around them was shuddering in time to a constant thudding sound.

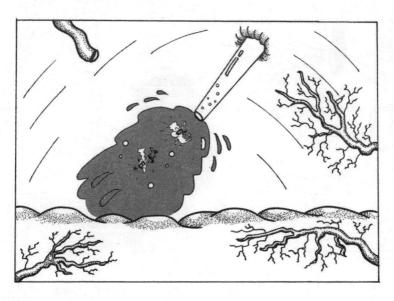

'Where are we?' asked Knowledge nervously. 'And what's that noise? We seem to be in some sort of nightclub.'

'Forget dancing, Knowledge,' said Captain Fact.

'That noise tells me we're in the Boss's heart. Follow me. Let's see if our virus is hiding in here.'

'I'm not sure if I like the heart,' said Knowledge. 'It's damp, noisy and wobbly . . .'

'Well, you wouldn't last long without one,' said Captain Fact. 'Ker-Fact! The heart is the muscle that never sleeps. Every second for the whole of your life it's pumping oxygenated and nutrient-rich blood that keeps your body going.'

30

Wobbling their way around the ever-throbbing heart, the search was on for the mystery virus.

'It's a bit like being in a house,' said Captain Fact. 'There's four main rooms: the two atriums and the two ventricles. The connecting corridors are the arteries and the veins.'

'But no kitchen,' said Knowledge, 'I haven't had anything to eat since breakfast. Pancake-flavoured dog biscuits – yum!'

'This is no time to talk about breakfast,' said Captain Fact, as his heart began to flutter . . .

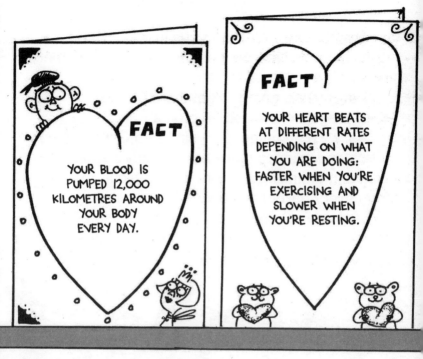

FACT

YOUR BLOOD IS PUMPED 12,000 KILOMETRES AROUND YOUR BODY EVERY DAY.

FACT

YOUR HEART BEATS AT DIFFERENT RATES DEPENDING ON WHAT YOU ARE DOING: FASTER WHEN YOU'RE EXERCISING AND SLOWER WHEN YOU'RE RESTING.

FACT

EVERY HEART IS A SLIGHTLY DIFFERENT SIZE, BUT IN ADULTS IT'S NORMALLY ABOUT THE SIZE OF A GRAPEFRUIT. IN KIDS IT'S ABOUT THE SIZE OF YOUR FIST.

ATTACK!!!

'There's no sign of the virus in here,' said Captain Fact. 'Next we need to check out another muscle.'

'How are we going to get there?' asked Knowledge. 'Are we jumping on a train?'

'No, we're jumping in a vein,' said Captain Fact. 'Veins and arteries make up the body's super-speed inter-linking network, taking blood to and from every part of the body.'

Captain Fact and Knowledge leapt into an artery and were soon being pumped at great speed in the direction of the boss's arm.

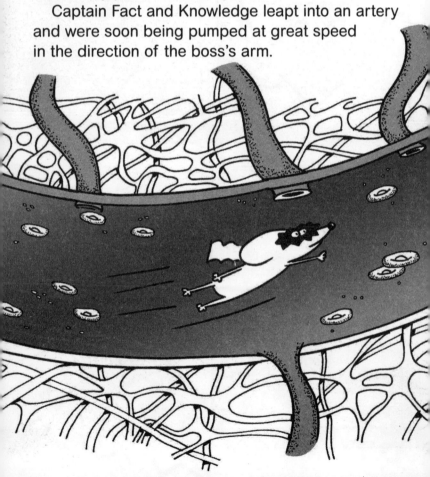

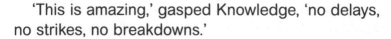

'This is amazing,' gasped Knowledge, 'no delays, no strikes, no breakdowns.'

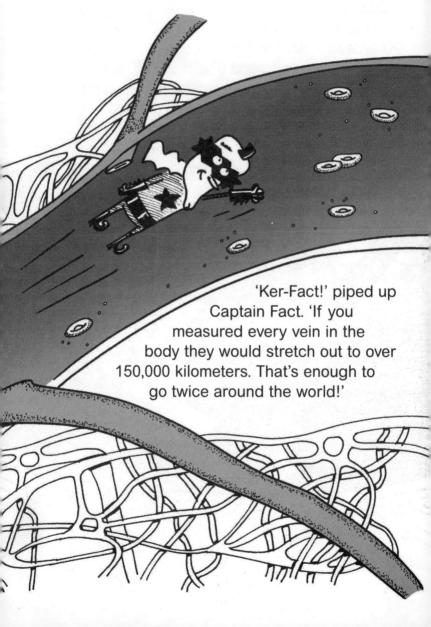

'Ker-Fact!' piped up Captain Fact. 'If you measured every vein in the body they would stretch out to over 150,000 kilometers. That's enough to go twice around the world!'

'Follow me, Knowledge,' continued Captain Fact. 'By my calculations the next capillary on the left should take us to the Boss's right arm muscle.'

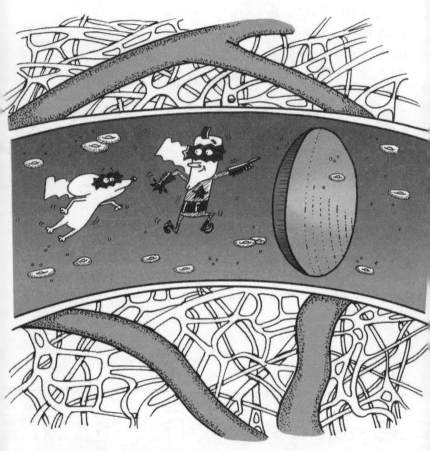

Taking a sharp left turn our two superheroes were ready to resume their search for the superbug . . .

CHAPTER 4
MUSCLE BOUND

'IT'S A BIT flabby in here,' said Knowledge, 'I thought muscles were meant to be lean and mean.'

'Well, it's the *Boss's* arm muscles,' said Captain Fact. 'All he does is lift up slices of pizza and occasionally wave a finger at us.'

'The Boss needs to get down to the gym and grow some big new muscles like mine,' said Knowledge as he flexed his doggie biceps.

'You don't get new muscles by exercising,' said Captain Fact. 'You just build up your existing ones.' And with that his triceps began to tickle . . .

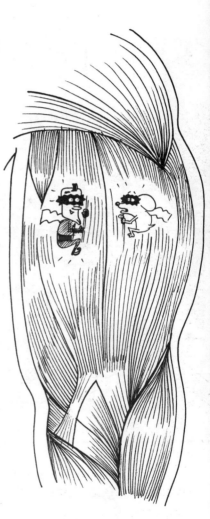

Without further ado Captain Fact was leading Knowledge up a tendon onto the Boss's arm bone.

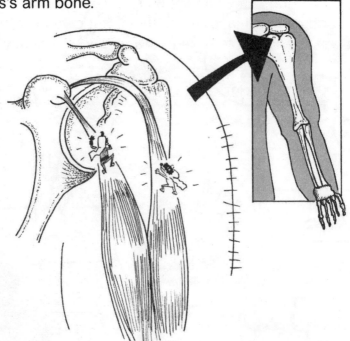

'We're in the Boss's humerus,' said Captain Fact.

'It's not very funny,' said Knowledge looking at the white walls around them.

'It's not meant to be funny: humerus is the name of the upper arm bone,' said Captain Fact. 'Ker-Fact! There are 206 bones in the human body. The biggest is the femur – that connects your hip to your kneecap – and the smallest is the stapes – a teeny-weeny bone in your inner ear.'

'I'm not like other dogs. I've always found bones really boring,' said Knowledge snootily. 'I know most dogs chew on them all day long, bury them and even fall in love with them. But give me a raspberry-ripple-flavoured dog biscuit *any* day.'

'There's nothing boring about bones, Knowledge,' said Captain Fact. 'Without them we'd be as wobbly as blancmanges. Not just that, bones are vital for all kinds of jobs,' he continued as he scanned for viruses. 'They act as levers for picking things up and walking. They protect softer body parts like the heart, lungs and the brain. And bone marrow in the middle of bones produces blood cells.'

'I still think I prefer dog biscuits,' mused Knowledge.

With no sign of the virus, Captain Fact and Knowledge took the plunge into an artery heading north.

CHAPTER 5
BRAIN STRAIN

IN NO TIME at all, Captain Fact and Knowledge were in the jugular vein zooming straight to the Boss's brain.

'Now!' shouted Captain Fact as they took a hard left. Our two superheroes landed on the mushy surface of the Boss's brain.

'Are you sure we're not in the stomach?' asked Knowledge looking around at the grey, jelly-like surface. 'It looks like cold porridge.'

'That's the cerebrum,' said Captain Fact getting his bearings. 'It's the largest part of the brain.'

As Captain Fact cautiously tiptoed along the cerebrum, Knowledge marched on noisily.

'Keep it down, Knowledge,' whispered Captain Fact urgently.

'What do you mean?' asked Knowledge. 'The Boss is out cold. There's nothing going on in here.'

'That's just where you're wrong,' said Captain Fact. 'The brain never goes to sleep.'

'Well, what does it do?' asked Knowledge, unconvinced.

'It's keeps the heart beating, the lungs breathing and the stomach digesting,' said Captain Fact. 'It tells you when to wake up and it also processes and stores memories from what's happened during the day.'

'I'm sure I just heard it shout *THORNHILL*!' joked Knowledge.

But Captain Fact's head was already starting to bulge . . .

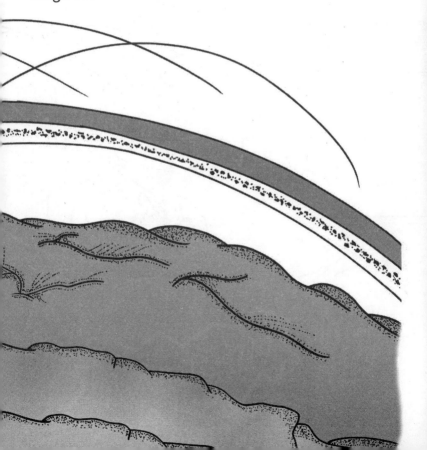

With no sign of the virus it was time to move on, but for once in his career Captain Fact was dawdling.

'What's going on?' asked Knowledge.

'Sorry, Knowledge, I just wanted to spend some quality time looking at the Boss's hippocampus,' said Captain Fact affectionately.

'Hippo what?' asked Knowledge.

'Hippocampus – it's the part of the brain where Facts are stored!'

After a final loving look, they were off in search of the superbug.

CHAPTER 6
EAR WE GO!

TWO VEINS AND a capillary later Captain Fact and Knowledge found themselves in the Boss's ear, up to their knees in a yellow gooey substance.

'Custard!' shouted Knowledge joyously. 'As much as you can eat! I've heard the legend of the Lost Canals of Custard, and here they are.'

'You don't want to eat that,' interrupted Captain Fact. 'It's earwax. Ker-Fact! Earwax coats the skin of the ear canal and acts as a temporary water repellent.'

'Yuk!' said Knowledge. 'I'll never be able to eat custard again.'

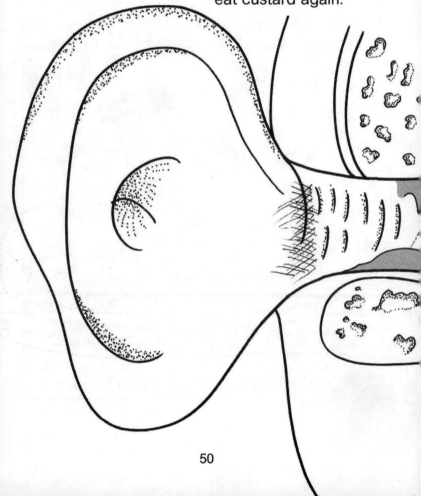

Captain Fact and Knowledge waded deeper into the ear canal. At the far end was a large circular pink disc blocking their path.

'That's the eardrum,' said Captain Fact.

'Eardrum? How are we going to get through that?' asked Knowledge.

'Hmmm . . . hang on a second, there's a tiny hole in it,' said Captain Fact. 'It would appear the Boss has a perforated eardrum. That would explain his shouting – he's hard of hearing.'

'Are you sure it's not just because he doesn't like us?' asked Knowledge.

But Captain Fact wasn't listening as his ears began to tingle . . .

'Still no virus,' said Captain Fact, 'follow me to the nose!'

Slipping through the hole in the Boss's eardrum Captain Fact and Knowledge made their way through the winding pipes and passages of the inner ear and into the air tube that led to the throat and on to the nose.

'We're in the nasal cavity, Knowledge,' said Captain Fact. 'Knowledge?'

But Knowledge had slipped on some snot and was sliding rapidly towards the Boss's left nostril!

'Grab a nose hair!' shouted Captain Fact.

At the last second Knowledge reached out and caught hold of one of the Boss's many dangling nasal hairs.

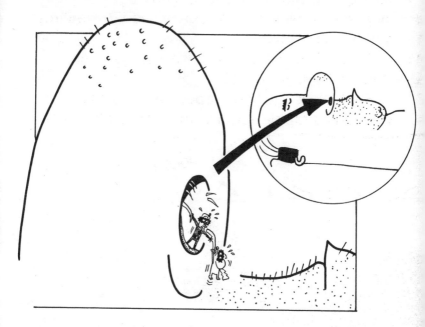

'Hold my hand!' shouted Captain Fact, reaching out for Knowledge. 'Fortunately the nose is full of hairs. They're here to trap and filter out bigger particles that get sniffed up.'

'I'm snot-soaked,' moaned Knowledge shaking himself off. 'Well, I think the nose stinks!'

'Funny you should say that,' said Captain Fact as his nostrils began to flare . . .

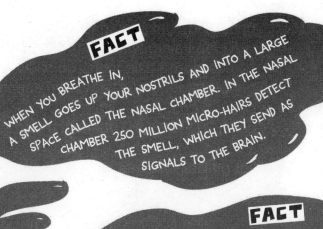

FACT

WHEN YOU BREATHE IN, A SMELL GOES UP YOUR NOSTRILS AND INTO A LARGE SPACE CALLED THE NASAL CHAMBER. IN THE NASAL CHAMBER 250 MILLION MICRO-HAIRS DETECT THE SMELL, WHICH THEY SEND AS SIGNALS TO THE BRAIN.

FACT

THE LINING OF THE NOSE ALSO ACTS AS A FILTER. TINY PARTICLES OF DUST AND GERMS GET STUCK TO IT SO THE AIR YOU BREATHE IS CLEANER. THESE END UP BECOMING BOGEYS!

FACT

THE NOSE CAN IDENTIFY MORE THAN 10,000 DIFFERENT SMELLS, FROM DELICATE PERFUMES TO STONKING GREAT STINKS!

ATTACK!!!

'I'll never sniff at the nose again,' said Knowledge.

'Good,' said Captain Fact. 'But the virus isn't here. Let's have a look in the Boss's mouth . . . all kinds of things lurk there.'

Captain Fact and Knowledge dashed to the back of the nasal cavity and followed the air passages that connect to the mouth.

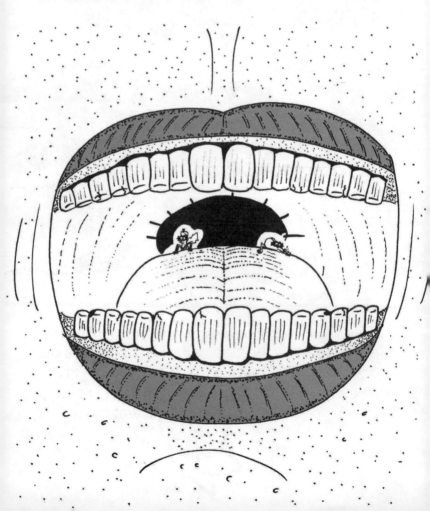

CHAPTER 7
THE BOSS BITES BACK

IN NO TIME at all, Captain Fact and Knowledge found themselves perched on a molar, scanning for viruses. But all they could see were bits of decomposing food and mouldy old fillings.

'This is really disgusting. And it's beginning to rain,' whinged Knowledge. 'You didn't predict that!'

'That's not rain, Knowledge, that's saliva. For once the Boss is literally drooling over us,' said Captain Fact as his mouth began to water . . .

FACT
TASTE BUDS ARE MAINLY ALONG THE EDGES OF THE TONGUE: SWEET FLAVOURS AT THE TIP, SALTY ONES ALONG THE FRONT SIDES, SOUR ONES ALONG THE REAR SIDES AND BITTER ONES ACROSS THE BACK.
FACT
YOUR TEETH ARE THE HARDEST PART OF YOUR BODY - AND THEY HAVE TO BE BECAUSE THEY SPEND A LIFETIME CHOMPING, NIBBLING, GNASHING AND CHEWING.
ATTACK!!!

All of a sudden there was a rumbling and Captain Fact noticed that the Boss's teeth were closing in on them.

'Duck!' shouted Captain Fact as he instinctively held up his arms, 'The Boss is about to grind his teeth! I don't think I can hold out any longer!'

Captain Fact's arms shuddered under the weight of the Boss's grinding jaws. 'The Fact Watch! Press the Emergency Button on the Fact Watch!'

Suddenly Factorella appeared, clinging to the end of a toothpick.

'Hello, guys! Wow, this place is amazing! But check out the dog breath! Sorry, Knowledge! And look at the yucky teeth! I bet the last time the Boss went to the dentist was when his mum took him. Gross!' exclaimed Factorella.

Captain Fact's knees were about to give way and all he could do was let out a high-pitched squeal.

'Whoops! Almost forgot – I'm here to rescue you aren't I?' said Factorella and with that she produced a jack, a bit like the one you'd use to change a tyre on a car. 'Dad built the Micro-Jack especially for an emergency like this.'

'Phew! Thanks, Factorella,' said Captain Fact, wiping the sweat from his brow, 'I thought I'd bitten off more that I could chew there.'

'You'd better keep looking for the virus,' said Factorella. 'Doctors still haven't found the cure! And more boils than ever are breaking out everywhere.'

'We'll get that virus,' said Captain Fact defiantly.

'I'd love to stick around but Dad wants me to get back and fix the toaster,' said Factorella, hopping back on the toothpick as it was pulled out of the Boss's mouth.

CHAPTER 8
FAR FLUNG LUNG

THERE WAS ONLY JUST time to wave Factorella goodbye before Captain Fact and Knowledge resumed their search.

'Have you noticed the nasty smell in here?' asked Captain Fact, as he walked to the back of the Boss's mouth.

'Yes, the smell of three-week-old pizza and rotting ice cream,' said Knowledge. 'It seems to come and go.'

'It's the Boss's breath,' said Captain Fact. 'Hold on to your cape, we're parachuting into his lungs!'

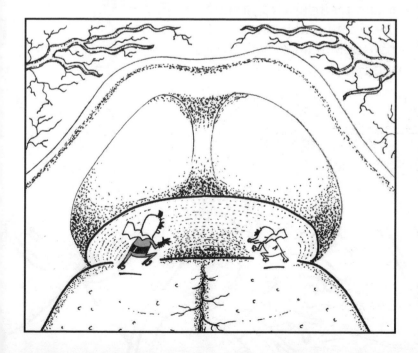

Captain Fact and Knowledge plunged down the Boss's windpipe.

'What was that trapdoor we just flew through?' asked Knowledge, who was starting to enjoy paragliding.

'It's the epiglottis,' said Captain Fact. 'Ker-Fact! The epiglottis stops food going down the windpipe and diverts it into the stomach. Hold tight, we're going into one of the bronchi!'

Captain Fact and Knowledge found themselves flying down the right-hand bronchus, a passage that led straight into the Boss's right lung!

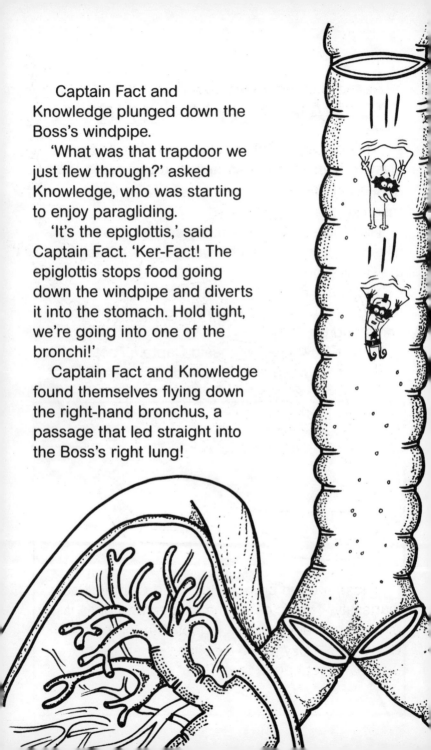

As they landed on the spongy surface of a lung they noticed millions of air passages all around them.

'This place is a bit spooky,' said Knowledge dusting himself down. 'It feels like tree-roots closing in on us.'

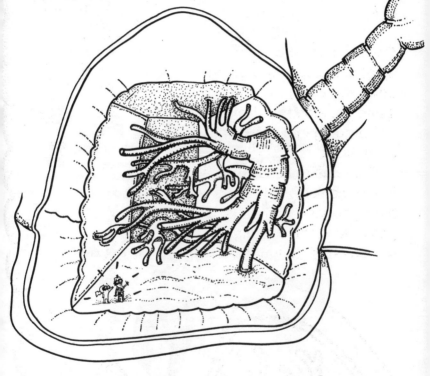

'Those are the bronchioles,' said Captain Fact fearlessly. 'They pick up the oxygen and pass it through air sacks before it goes into the blood. Blood needs oxygen to function . . .' And with that his chest began to puff out . . .

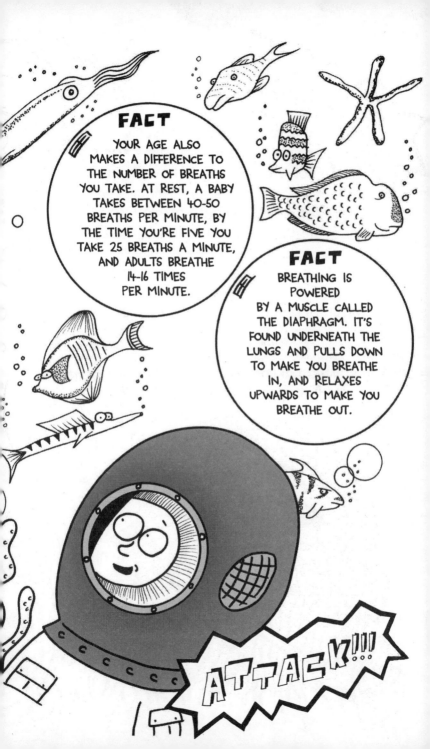

FACT

YOUR AGE ALSO MAKES A DIFFERENCE TO THE NUMBER OF BREATHS YOU TAKE. AT REST, A BABY TAKES BETWEEN 40-50 BREATHS PER MINUTE, BY THE TIME YOU'RE FIVE YOU TAKE 25 BREATHS A MINUTE, AND ADULTS BREATHE 14-16 TIMES PER MINUTE.

FACT

BREATHING IS POWERED BY A MUSCLE CALLED THE DIAPHRAGM. IT'S FOUND UNDERNEATH THE LUNGS AND PULLS DOWN TO MAKE YOU BREATHE IN, AND RELAXES UPWARDS TO MAKE YOU BREATHE OUT.

ATTACK!!!

Despite searching every corner of the Boss's lungs there was still no sign of the virus.

'We need to get out of here quickly to carry on the search,' said Captain Fact. 'It's time to use the Power of Fact. We're going to have to be coughed out!'

'Coughed out! Yuk!' said Knowledge.

'Get coated in the Boss's mucus, then irritate the tiny hairs, called cilias, surrounding us,' said Captain Fact as he started to cover himself in the sticky goo. 'Ker-Fact! Cilias sweep dirty mucus to the throat to be coughed out. That's where we want to go.'

With our two superheroes plastered in mucus they started tickling the walls of the Boss's lung. Before long the whole place was wobbling and juddering . . .

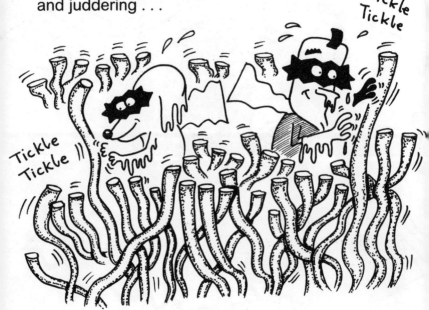

CHAPTER 9
A SPOT OF BOTHER

THERE WAS A huge explosion as the Boss coughed and Captain Fact and Knowledge were hurtled back up the airwaves and out through his mouth. With a huge squelch they splattered onto the Boss's chin.

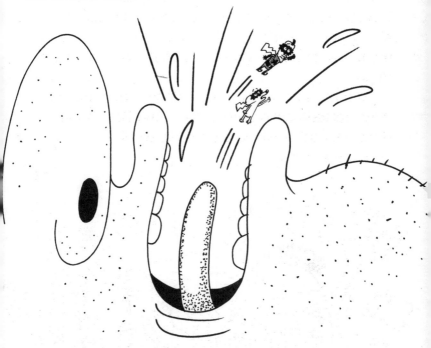

'Shake yourself down, Knowledge,' said Captain Fact, flicking mucus from his gloves. 'Let's check the Boss's skin for the virus.'

'It's like being on the surface of a weird planet,' observed Knowledge as they wove their way between giant hairs. 'And look, there's a bouncy castle.'

As Knowledge leapt up and down on the soft yellow-and-red bulge, Captain Fact winced.

'I'd get off that if I were you,' said Captain Fact. 'It's not a bouncy castle, it's *acne vulgaris*, more commonly known as a zit!'

But it was too late. Much to Captain Fact's amusement, the zit erupted, showering Knowledge in yellow pus.

Captain Fact laughed so hard he fell over backwards into a shaving cut.

Now it was Knowledge's turn to have a laugh, but Captain Fact seemed to be enjoying himself: 'It's amazing in here, Knowledge!' he shouted. 'I can see all the different layers of the skin.' And with that his chin began to itch . . .

FACT

FACT

THE SKIN IS THE LARGEST ORGAN OF THE BODY.

FACT

SKIN IS MADE UP OF TWO LAYERS: THE EPIDERMIS IS THE THIN OUTER LAYER MADE UP OF DEAD SKIN CELLS, AND THE DERMIS IS THE THICKER BOTTOM LAYER.

FACT

SKIN GIVES US OUR SENSE OF TOUCH. THE DERMIS CONTAINS MILLIONS OF SENSORS WHICH ARE JOINED BY NERVES TO THE BRAIN AND THESE DETECT EVERYTHING: HEAT, COLD AND, OF COURSE, PAIN.

"CAIRO DUSK"

EYE MAKEUP

Suddenly a colossal dome-shaped object loomed over them!

'I told you this place was like a weird planet!' whined Knowledge. 'Now the moon's heading straight for us!'

'It's not the moon, it's Professor Miniscule,' said Captain Fact.

Professor Miniscule seemed agitated. His voice boomed across the Boss's chin. 'The virus is getting out of control!' he shouted. 'Doctors are certain it's to be found somewhere in the digestive system. You must get swallowed at once!'

76

CHAPTER 10
GUT FEELING

WITH RENEWED DETERMINATION our two superheroes charged to the back of the Boss's mouth.

'We need to trigger the swallowing reflex,' said Captain Fact. Then he asked the question Knowledge always dreaded: 'Do you have any dog biscuits?'

'Only one,' wheedled Knowledge, 'it's marrow-bone-and-chocolate-chip flavoured, I was saving it for—' But before he could finish his sentence Captain Fact had grabbed it and was waving it at the back of the Boss's throat. In no time at all the Boss was salivating and started to swallow . . .

'Hold tight!' shouted Captain Fact, as his belly began to rumble . . .

THE DIGESTION PROCESS STARTS AS SOON AS YOU TAKE YOUR FIRST BITE:

WHAT'S LEFT OVER GOES INTO THE LARGE INTESTINE, WHERE ANY WATER IS RE-ABSORBED BY THE BODY. WHAT'S LEFT OVER IS POO!

FACT

CAPTAIN FACT'S

IN THE SMALL INTESTINE MORE JUICES FROM THE LIVER AND PANCREAS GET TO WORK ON THE FOOD, BREAKING IT DOWN INTO 'NUTRIENTS'. THESE NUTRIENTS ARE ABSORBED THROUGH THE WALLS OF THE SMALL INTESTINE INTO THE BLOODSTREAM TO BE USED BY THE BODY.

YOUR MOUTH STARTS TO WATER WITH SALIVA, WHICH CONTAINS CHEMICALS THAT BREAK DOWN FOOD AND HELP YOU SWALLOW.

YOUR TEETH GRIND THE FOOD AND YOUR TONGUE SQUASHES IT UP AND PUSHES IT TO THE BACK OF YOUR THROAT TO BE SWALLOWED. SWALLOWED FOOD PASSES THROUGH THE OESOPHAGUS...

ATTACK!!!!

...WHERE IT IS SQUEEZED INTO A LONG THIN SHAPE, A BIT LIKE TOOTHPASTE, BEFORE PASSING INTO YOUR STOMACH.

DIGESTIVE JUICES

Having plummeted down the oesophagus, Captain Fact and Knowledge found themselves in the stomach.

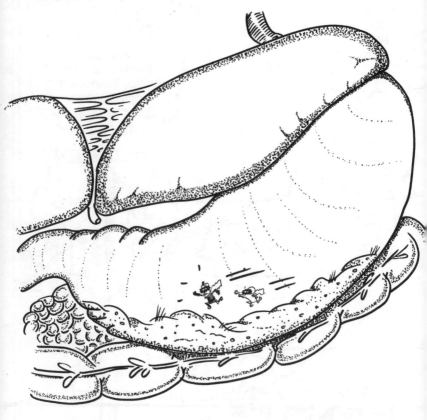

'What's going on?' asked Knowledge. 'We're being churned, squeezed and it's raining acid.'

'We're being digested,' said Captain Fact ominously. 'We can't hang around in here or we'll be dissolved and absorbed!'

From the stomach into the duodenum
Captain Fact and Knowledge searched
desperately for the virus.

'What's this
horrible looking
mush?' asked Knowledge.

'The Boss's breakfast by the looks of things,'
said Captain Fact, 'the acids and enzymes are
breaking it down. I can still make out bacon, egg
and . . . fried squid!'

From the small intestine into the large intestine things were getting smellier, but still no sign of a superbug . . .

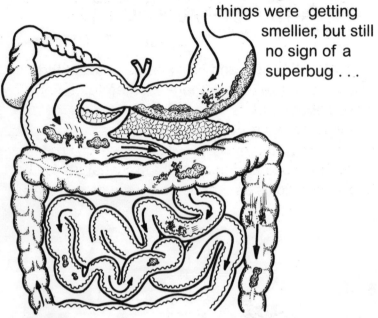

'From the way we're getting squeezed I think we'll soon be turned into poo,' warned Captain Fact.

'Earwax, saliva, snot, mucus, pus and now poo,' wailed Knowledge.

'But no virus,' said Captain Fact despairingly.

'Oh well,' sighed Knowledge, 'we'd best be on our way. All of this time in the stomach has given me an appetite. We gave it our best shot.'

'A superhero never gives up!' said Captain Fact. Just then, out of the corner of his eye he spotted a small opening . . .

CHAPTER 11
VIRAL VENDETTA

AS CAPTAIN FACT and Knowledge entered the small, worm-like tunnel, there seemed to be some movement ahead.

'We're entering the appendix,' whispered Captain Fact nervously. 'Ker-Fact! It serves no known purpose and nobody knows what it's for. I had appendicitis as a child so mine was removed.'

But before Captain Fact could go into the details of his operation, they turned a corner . . .

THERE WERE VIRUSES EVERYWHERE!

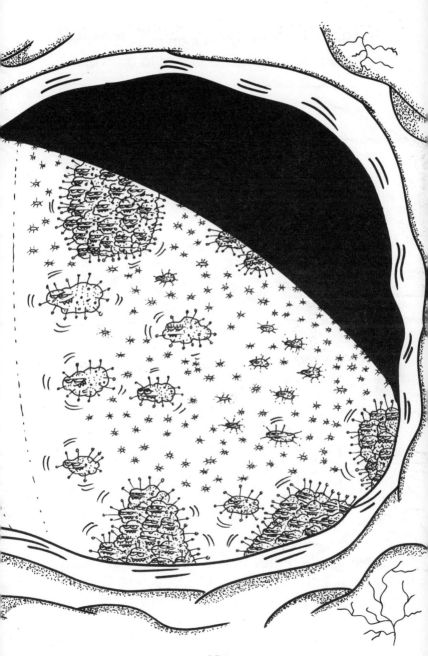

'So this is where they're lurking!' said Captain Fact. 'Quick, Knowledge, we need to grab one!'

Having wrestled a virus to the ground Captain Fact used the Fact Watch to scan the surly superbug. Then they beat a hasty retreat from the appendix into the large intestine, where Captain Fact finally made contact with Professor Miniscule.

'Congratulations, Captain Fact!' crackled Professor Miniscule. 'So they were in the appendix. I should have guessed.'

'It explains why not everyone has come down with the illness,' said Captain Fact.

'Exactly!' said Professor Miniscule. 'We've both had our appendix out so we're fine. I've informed the medical authorities and, with the information from your scanned virus, they should have an inoculation ready in no time! Once again, you've saved the world!'

'Great! Now, how are we going to get out of here?' asked Captain Fact. 'We've got the evening weather forecast to do.'

'Head to the rectum and I'll explain,' replied Professor Miniscule.

As the two superheroes dashed to the rectum, Captain Fact's bottom began to wobble . . .

FACT

DRINKING – YOU'RE 60% WATER SO KEEP YOURSELF TOPPED UP. YOU CAN SURVIVE ABOUT A MONTH WITHOUT FOOD BUT ONLY 5-7 DAYS WITHOUT WATER!

FACT

SLEEPING – THE BODY NEEDS REST. A BABY NEEDS 16 HOURS OF SLEEP A DAY, A TEENAGER NEEDS ABOUT 9, AND AN ADULT 7-8 HOURS.

Zzzzz

FACT

EATING – IT'S IMPORTANT TO HAVE A BALANCED DIET, AND THAT DOESN'T MEAN THE SAME AMOUNT OF CHOCOLATE AS DOUGHNUTS! MAKE SURE YOU HAVE FOODS FROM THE FIVE FOOD GROUPS: FRUIT AND VEG, MEAT AND FISH, DAIRY, CEREALS AND POTATOES, AND LAST - AND WHAT SHOULD BE LEAST - FATTY AND SUGARY FOODS.

FACT

EXERCISE – WATCHING TV AND PLAYING VIDEO GAMES DOESN'T EXERCISE YOUR BODY. ACTIVITY KEEPS YOUR MUSCLES, BONES AND JOINTS IN GOOD SHAPE AND IS GREAT FOR YOUR HEART AND LUNGS.

ATTACK!!!

FACT

GERMS - THEY'RE EVERYWHERE, OFTEN IN THE MOST UNEXPECTED PLACES. THERE ARE MORE GERMS ON A TELEPHONE RECEIVER THAN A TOILET SEAT! TO MINIMIZE CONTACT WITH THESE DISEASE-CARRYING CRITTERS WASH YOUR HANDS AFTER YOU'VE BEEN TO THE LOO AND BEFORE MEALS . . . AND DON'T DUCK OUT OF BATH TIME!

FACT

SKIN - THE SUN CAN BE DANGEROUS AS IT CONTAINS POTENTIALLY HARMFUL ULTRA VIOLET LIGHT! IF IT'S HOT, SLIP ON A HAT, SLAP ON A T-SHIRT AND SLOP ON SOME SUNSCREEN - AND REMEMBER SHADE IS GOOD!

FACT

STIMULATION - DON'T FORGET YOUR BRAIN! KEEP IT ACTIVE WITH LOTS OF READING.

Once Captain Fact and Knowledge were in the Boss's rectum, Professor Miniscule crackled through on the Fact Watch again.

'Listen up team! I'm going to un-shrink you by remote control. The Boss has been taken back to his office for his inoculation and on the way he's been fed a full Tex Mex platter: spicy beans, chilli con carne and an extra hot burrito.'

'Does this mean what I think it means?' asked Captain Fact nervously.

'Yes,' replied Professor Miniscule. 'Get your masks off and hold on to your noses, any second now all of that hot and spicy food should trigger an emission of methane gas.'

'Oh, no!' wailed Knowledge. 'We're going to be farted ouuuuuuuuuuuuuut!'

CHAPTER 12
AND NOW THE WEATHER . . .

CAPTAIN FACT AND Knowledge shook and shuddered before they were quite literally blown out of the Boss's bottom. There was a loud bang as Miniscule instantaneously un-shrunk them by remote control.

KA-FAART!

'What's going on!?!' shouted the Boss, 'I'm sure I just saw Thornhill and Puddles crawl out from underneath my wheelchair. I need medication!!!'

But Cliff and Puddles were running as fast as they could back to their office.

'Good thing I had a shower installed,' said Cliff scrubbing himself down.

'I still feel dirty,' said Puddles and he shuddered at the thought of the various bodily fluids they'd encountered. 'It wouldn't have been so bad if it hadn't been the Boss.'

Freshly showered, Cliff Thornhill and Puddles entered the Make-up Department.

'There you are,' said Lucy, 'I've been looking all over for you. Captain Fact found the virus and now they've got a cure!'

'Really?' said Cliff, trying not to give away his identity.

'Yes, he's amazing,' gushed Lucy. 'Captain Fact always gets *my* heart pumping.'

Cliff blushed as they stepped in front of the cameras.

And so, with a global epidemic of bottom boils averted, Cliff Thornhill and Puddles were safely back doing what they did worst – the weather.

Until the next crisis . . .

CAPTAIN FACT's

SPACE ADVENTURE
DINOSAUR ADVENTURE
CREEPY-CRAWLY
ADVENTURE

AND

EGYPTIAN ADVENTURE

ARE AVAILABLE IN
BOOKSHOPS NOW!

COMING SOON!

ROMAN ADVENTURE